BIKER'S SECRET TWINS

BWWM Mafia Romance

Jolie Damman

ISBN: 9798842477692
Imprint: Independently published

1st edition

Cover design by: Jolie Damman

CONTENTS

Title Page

Copyright

Chapter 1   1

Chapter 2   5

Chapter 3   8

Chapter 4   11

Chapter 5   14

Chapter 6   18

Chapter 7   22

Chapter 8   25

Chapter 9   28

Chapter 10   31

Chapter 11   34

Chapter 12   38

Chapter 13   42

Chapter 14   45

Chapter 15   48

Chapter 16   52

Fred's Epilogue   55

Madeine's Epilogue   58

Teaser: Biker's Lost Baby   63

Similar Books 67

About the Author 69

CHAPTER 1

Madeine

I had no idea what I was doing. Someone like him was obviously off-limits, and yet I kept on thinking that something was going to happen between us. Why did I think that? Because he was absolutely, undoubtedly smoking hot, and just looking at him was enough to make me feel some wetness in my pussy.

He was standing in front of me, and he was so close that I could almost smell the breath coming out of his mouth.

He had me cornered against the wall, and I couldn't move, couldn't go anywhere. My boyfriend could see me doing this, and he would be pissed. He would be so angry that the first thing he would do would be to pull out his gun and shoot at this handsome man standing in front of me.

He looked like the opposite of a star. He was rugged, a little dirty, rough, and muscular, and he had thick, dense hair on his chest, which was one of the things about him that most stood out. I couldn't stop looking down and... admiring it. It just made my nipples so hard.

It made me feel increased wetness in my pussy, and I soon found myself pressing my legs together, as though I was afraid that he was going to impale himself between them if I wasn't doing it.

I knew that it was a silly thought, especially because he would never do anything to me that I didn't want. Even though I had an okay relationship with my boyfriend, recently he had begun to show me that he didn't care much about me.

He didn't care much about my issues, and this man standing right here, holding the beer can in his hand, was beginning to show me that he was so much better.

So much more like a real man.

He was taller than me, so much so that I could imagine myself putting my arms around his body and letting him put his chin on top of my head, something I was certain he was also thinking about.

"Someone like you shouldn't have been left alone like this. A man like me might steal you," he threatened, making me hate him more than I already did.

It didn't matter how hot he was, he was always going to make me feel irritated with his snarky comments. He was always so assured of himself, and that was something that would never change.

My body was beginning to get hotter. I had to do something about it, but I couldn't. Again, I remembered that he had me cornered against the wall.

I could only hear the pounding music coming from behind me, reminding me that the party was still going strong.

"I'm not going to let you do that. It doesn't matter how hot, how important, how smart, and how pretty much everything else you think you are, you are not going to make me cheat on my boyfriend."

"Is that so?" He asked, brushing his finger on my cheek, and I could almost feel myself physically recoiling, but I didn't do it because I didn't want to show weakness, especially not in front of someone with such a high opinion of himself.

"That's right. It's something that you can't change about us, and you need to start to get used to it."

He curled up the right corner of his lips. "You are always trying to be so tough, but in the end, you are nothing more than a girl that needs to shut up and do exactly everything I want. I'm above your boyfriend when it comes to pretty much everything, and that's also something that will never be changed."

"I don't care. I'm with James and that's everything that matters," I tried to say, trying to push him away with my hand, but it didn't work. Fred didn't budge. I knew that he wasn't going to, especially after emptying a few beer cans.

He wasn't drunk, but he was still totally unhinged. He was much bolder right now, to the point of brushing his fingers on my cheek, which he was doing again.

I lifted my hand. I was going to slap his face to show him that I wasn't kidding. Not to mention that he should be feeling ashamed of himself. What the hell was he thinking could even happen between us that wouldn't usher a catastrophe to the motorcycle club? Was he thinking about fully destroying it, especially after everything that happened under Harry's leadership?

He was the former president of the biker club and also its founder. He was the one that established everything, but now he was living far away from the country. It was Fred, a.k.a. 'Promise', that had picked up the pieces and melded them together.

It meant that the motorcycle club was 'back in shape' but it was still far from enough to instill fear in the other motorcycle club members, something I was sure that he didn't like one bit.

Having drunk a little tonight, I was also beginning to feel that I was a little unhinged. I mean, what was I even thinking was going to happen between us? I didn't know, but standing here in the middle of this hallway, where everybody could see us, just wasn't doing me any favors, and I was beginning to grow paranoid that my whole life was going to be ruined.

It was with that thought in mind that I stated incisively, "You need to leave. I need to go back to my boyfriend, go back to James, and we need to pretend that this never happened."

And this time, I could feel my rage bubbling in my veins. I just wanted to punch his face until he was asking for my forgiveness, but I knew how pointless that would be, especially because he was so much stronger than me. Not to mention that he was growing bolder as time passed, and I knew he was about to do something stupid.

I could see him lowering his head.

I couldn't do anything about it, especially when our lips finally connected. I knew that I should be slapping his face until he was recoiling away from me, but that was so difficult, especially when his lips were so sweet. So good. So tender, and the kiss was a lot more than I thought it would be.

There was no denying that Fred was a good kisser.

CHAPTER 2

Fred

I couldn't stop kissing Madeine. Her lips were so sweet, so hot, so tender and this was hands down one of the best kisses of my life, and I couldn't see myself ever kissing someone else and thinking that it was the same thing. It just wouldn't be.

And I knew I was making a big mistake because her boyfriend was also my friend. He was also my second-in-command, and I was well aware of the possible ramifications of my choice.

But it was so difficult to be thinking about them when everything was going so right for me, and especially when she was melting under my dominance. I could feel her body melting. I could feel it just giving up, and it was everything I needed to know.

It was everything so that I could make the kiss hotter, longer, more passionate, wetter, and she was letting all of that just happen.

When I broke the kiss, however, she looked at me as though she wanted to kill me. But even though that was the case, I felt the opposite. I felt that I wanted to be with Madeine for the rest of my life, something so silly but which also rang so true to me.

"You are such an asshole," she barked and if she were to try to slap me again, I would be ready for it. I would be ready to grab her wrist in case she tried to do that, and… thankfully she didn't.

"I know I am, but you still like me for the way I am, don't you?" I said, moving my hand over the side of her body. If she didn't stop me now, I would be touching her boob and perhaps even doing a lot more than that.

She bit her bottom lip. Even though her relationship with James used to be better, she just would never admit the truth, especially not in front of me.

"I shouldn't be doing this," she said, breathless, ducking under my right arm and then running away from me so quickly I didn't have enough time to stop her. In a moment, she was going upstairs, to the second floor, and I had to run after her.

I tossed my beer can over my shoulder. The beer was good, but it didn't matter right now. What mattered was finding her, being with her, and that I was going to make it all happen right at this moment.

Madeine was about to shut the door right in my face when I put my hand against it, stopping her. She glared at me. She wanted to kill me right now, especially because she just wanted to be away from everything bad that was tormenting her mind.

But it was all pointless. There was a solution and I was it.

"You're not going to get away from me so easily, Madeine," I promised, pushing the door until it was open, and I stepped inside the room, finding myself right with her. I had never been in this room, and there was almost something peculiar about it that I couldn't put my finger on.

"Get away from me, you monster. I'm going to kill you. You want to ruin my relationship with James, but it's not going to work."

I stopped where I was. I wasn't going to do anything against her will, especially because I wanted to take my time with her. I knew I was doing something wrong, but it was impossible to control my urges, especially when Madeine looked so tempting.

Her perfect curves.

Her full lips.

Her long, black hair, and pretty much everything about her made me feel my dick giving somersaults under my pants. I was hard. There was no denying it. The only thing I wanted to be doing right now was to be diving between her legs, and I knew she wanted the same.

After all, Madeine just couldn't stop flicking her eyes down, assessing my body, checking me out, and eating me with her eyes.

"I'm not going anywhere. I know you want this. I know how much you want me."

And then, I waited for the confirmation I needed. Madeine didn't start to scream, didn't run, didn't start fighting against me, and just let me approach her. When I was right in front of her again, she almost started to cry.

"The truth is that… James has been so bad, so terrible to me, and I can't help but think that I made a huge mistake when I decided that we were going to get married."

I put my finger against her lips, stopping her from speaking any further.

"You don't need to worry about any of that or him. I'm here. I'm here for you, and whatever you need. Tonight, the only thing I want to do is to give you an amazing night, and I think that we can make that happen. I want to love you. I want to love your body, your curves, your tits, and pretty much everything about you.

She looked up at me with dreamy eyes. I knew what Madeine was thinking, but she wasn't going to say anything, and the only thing I needed right now was that she wasn't doing anything when I started to lift her shirt, finally revealing to the delight of my eyes her perfect, curvy, round breasts, and they were as tempting as I had thought they were.

Thus, I couldn't stop myself when I started to massage, fumble, feel, touch, and do everything else I was entitled to when she was finally giving herself up to me.

CHAPTER 3

Madeine

I knew I was making a mistake, but I couldn't stop it anymore. Fred was so hot, especially the way that his fingers were feeling me. Every part of me. My nipples, my breasts, my belly, and everything else.

It was such a pity that I couldn't do the same.

Why was I doing this? It was pretty obvious. My boyfriend didn't love me anymore, and I needed this. My life had been pretty stressful recently, and I needed something to make me have hope again that everything was going to be okay.

Fred's eyes were boring into mine. Their intensity. His gaze. The way that he was looking at me, it was like he was looking into my soul. His fingers were still touching me, and I couldn't do anything about it.

"You like it when I touch you like this, don't you?" Fred asked, his finger grazing over my nipple. Of course I liked it, but I wasn't going to say anything, especially because I didn't want him to think that what was happening tonight was something that was going to become frequent between us.

I bit my bottom lip. I refused to give Fred the answer he was seeking.

"This is going to end so badly."

"I know, but you don't need to worry. It's not like James will find out anything, and even if he does, I'll be ready to protect you against him," he promised, his eyes still boring into mine, and I knew he was telling me the truth.

He wasn't someone that usually told the truth, but right now he was, and I couldn't help but feel protected and increased wetness in my pussy.

He lowered his hand, pushing my pants down. He finished lowering them until I stepped out of them, and when I did, he had full access to my body. I felt his hands moving over my legs, feeling every part of them, every inch, and then he stopped when he was no more than mere moments from finding my pussy.

Of course, it was protected by my panties, but I figured that not even that was enough to stop him. And truly, it wasn't. The moment that I felt his finger grazing over my panties, he didn't stop, yanking them off me like they were nothing.

For someone like Fred, they might as well be.

His eyes looked down, finding my clit and pussy lips. He was enjoying what he was seeing, and he couldn't hide the smile that crept up his face.

"You're delicious. You are absolutely stunning, and it's such a pity that you have been waiting so long for the right man to show up and show you how right I am," he groaned, breathing on my neck, his lips dangerously close to kissing me, and I thought he really was going to, but in the end, he just pulled his head back. Of course he was going to tease me about doing that, which was like torture to me.

I was vulnerable, but I wasn't entirely defenseless. Having witnessed what he just did, I planted both of my hands on his cheeks, pulling his head down until we were kissing again.

And I thought he was going to feel pissed at that, but he didn't. I could tell that he was feeling the opposite. Fred was actually smiling back, and his smile was as devilish as it should be.

"You're really enjoying this, aren't you?" He asked, putting his tongue out and then flicking it on my earlobe, making my body shudder. It was incredible, the way he did that, sending shockwaves of pleasure through my body.

"I am, and I'm not going to lie," I said and then he put his hands on my shoulders, turning me around.

I couldn't believe that I just let him do that. I thought that I was going to be much more incisive about this, but it just wasn't happening, and then I felt his hands moving over my backside, and it was all over.

There was a mirror in front of me and it was big enough to let me see everything he was doing. It was a pity that he hadn't taken off his shirt yet. If there was something I wanted to be doing right now, it was seeing his perfect, big, and imposing torso without it, and I was certain that all my doubts would be squashed when that finally happened.

Unfortunately, it wasn't meant to be. Fred was entertained with something else, and that was seeing my naked behind. His fingers continued to explore every inch of me, and while I wasn't even moving my arms or my fingers, I felt his finger going into the crack of my ass, and then he looked for my anus.

When he found it, I thought that he was going to start to rub his finger on it, but I was mistaken about it. His eyes were looking at mine through the reflection in the mirror, and that smile on his face just refused to fade away. The evil thoughts swirling in his mind right now... It was more than obvious that he wanted to do something to me that we all knew was forbidden.

Then, he put his hands against my shoulders again and this time he pressed his body to mine, and I felt his hard-on against my buttocks. It was so much bigger than I had thought, and I didn't know what I should be doing. My body was beginning to tremble, and I knew that he had me under his complete control.

Thus, it was surprising when he stepped away from me, taking only some steps, and... I didn't do anything. He even said, "Don't move. Don't go anywhere. I'm watching everything you're doing, and that's not even the tip of the iceberg of it. That's how much I want you, and that's also how much I know you are enjoying what's happening right now."

And Fred was right. I felt so powerless that I couldn't even hope to stop him.

CHAPTER 4

Fred

Fuck, it was going to happen. I was going to fuck my friend's girlfriend, and he was completely oblivious to it. She was in front of me, in front of the mirror, and she was looking at me. She couldn't see my reflection and I could see, feel, and smell the wetness seeping out of her sopping wet cunt. Gosh, when I was inside of her, I promised that I was going to make tonight unforgettable.

"What are you waiting for?" She hissed, her fingers twitching. I loved the way that Madeine was showing her nervousness and anxiety. She just couldn't wait for a second longer, could she? I asked myself, but the answer was obvious.

"Don't worry, pretty little thing. I'm just taking my time, but what you want from me – it's happening right now," I promised, putting my fingers under the hem of my shirt and then lifting it up and over my head, tossing it behind me. It was unimportant right now, and we all knew that damn well.

When she could finally see my exposed, naked torso, I noticed the breath getting stuck in her throat. I almost wanted to go over there and help her unclog it, but it would be pointless. I knew that that was going to be happening so many more times, especially tonight. I said that because I was planning on making this something more frequent between us.

More one-night stands.

"Do you like it?" I asked, stepping toward her and then letting her turn around so that she could finally feel my body. And I felt her fingers roaming over my curves, my muscles, and every inch and part of me.

And I had to ask her a question I didn't even know how she was going to take. I knew it was a risk, but I was more than willing to face it, and I knew that she was thinking the same thing.

"Is it better than James'?" I finally asked, and then I noticed her breathing stopping, but only for a brief moment. She quickly regained control over her breathing, and everything was fine. Thank goodness, I thought. For a moment, I thought that she was going to pass out because she couldn't breathe anymore.

"I'm certainly not going to answer that."

I growled. I figured that her answer was to be expected, but it was still disappointing. I put my hands on her shoulders again, moving them over her backside, and then slipping my hand between her ass crack, parting her asscheeks.

She just let me do that without uttering a single complaint, and that was the green light that I needed, the go-ahead.

"How disappointing. I thought you had more in you than that."

"I'm not going to say anything about that, either."

I chuckled.

"Of course that you aren't. The only thing that you want to do right now is see my cock for the first time, isn't that right?" I asked, finding her eyes again, and for a moment she didn't say anything. I was almost disappointed again.

I was afraid that she was going to toss her clothes back on, and storm out of the room crying again, but thankfully... That didn't happen.

"I don't think I should say anything about that as well," she said, smiling.

"Then you might as well shut your lips for the rest of the night," I growled and it wasn't a recommendation, but rather an order – an order that she had to obey down to the letter, which I knew she was going to. Or she might not. She was always confrontational.

After a brief moment of silence, I took her until she was in front of the bed, and then I put my hand on her back again. I could feel how smooth, how soft, and how much everything her skin was, and I was in love with it. I couldn't stop feeling and exploring her tempting skin, and that was putting it mildly.

I guessed that her still being in her early twenties helped, I thought, saying, "Lie down on the bed. Since you don't want to say anything about anything, then you aren't going to see my cock. You are only going to feel it."

She gasped and then blinked twice, looking so submissive right now. While I was the dominant one, I was going to make tonight special for her. My fingers roamed, explored, felt, and did every other thing possible to her advantageous buttocks, and then I finally lowered my pants. Seconds later, I did the same with my pair of boxer briefs.

Having done that, my cock was finally free, and I could feel how much she wanted me inside of her. Her body was trembling just thinking about it. I was going to take my time, I thought, positioning myself on top of her and then putting on a condom.

Of course I was going to use a condom for this. The last thing I wanted was to get her pregnant and then have to deal with something I didn't want in my life: babies. I just didn't want babies in my life, much less a family.

This was nothing more than a one-night stand and it was going to remain that way, I thought, sliding my prick inside her pussy and then lodging myself in there and not thinking about stopping until she was crying out my name, something I was certain she was going to be doing in less than a couple of seconds.

I was still inside of her when I leaned down, positioning my lips by the side of her ear. "How does it feel to have your boyfriend's buddy inside of you? Great?" I asked, and I knew that she was going to give me the answer I wanted.

"It's so much better than I expected."

CHAPTER 5

Madeine

Fred was inside of me and everything he was doing was showing me that he was enjoying this as much as I was. When he was used to my size, my walls, and how they clenched around his prick, he started to roll his hips. His pace was slow at the beginning, which was just the way I liked it.

"Gosh, you are so tight," he said and him saying that, instead of making me feel anything else, made me feel so good about this. Yes, I was cheating on my boyfriend, who I knew had never cheated on me, and yet it was still so good to have someone that could finally make me feel like a woman, and that was exactly what he was doing.

I felt his hands going around me, looking for my breasts and while he fucked me, he played with them, played with my nipples, and with every inch of them that he could find, and it was making me feel breathless.

I knew that he was good when fucking a woman, but I didn't think that he was like this.

Fred was truly someone else.

"You're so big. I have no idea how I am taking this without it completely destroying me," I confessed, and I noticed that he was smiling, even though I couldn't see his face.

I just knew that he was smiling because it was obvious. Fred always had a high opinion of himself, and that would never change.

"I really hope you like it because I'm going to give you a lot more than this," he said, picking up the pace and showing me what he meant. He wanted to fuck me hard and he was doing just that.

The way that he was moving, thrusting, and pounding with his hips was beyond anything I thought possible, and I soon found myself matching him thrust for thrust.

It was exhilarating, and then I soon found myself crying out his name over and over.

It was a good thing that the music continued to pound through the walls of the house. Nobody could hear what we were doing, I reassured myself, vaguely remembering that I still had my boyfriend, but at the moment, he didn't matter one bit.

My pussy was wet. It was soaking wet, tight, warm, and it felt so stretched, so wide, and so pretty much every other thing.

The good thing was that I was on birth control, and there was no way that I would get pregnant from this. Fred had also put on his condom, thus further making sure that this was not going to end with me having his babies, something that comforted me right now.

I could feel his hands moving over my body.

He had picked up the pace and now I could also feel his balls slapping against my ass.

I could also feel how sweaty my body was.

We had achieved a rhythm that showed me that this was about to end, and then I soon found myself moaning, groaning, and spurring him on, incentivizing him to reach his climax, which I knew he was going to.

It was only a couple of moments later when I felt his prick twitching and erupting inside of me. When he did that, he started to huff, groan, and moan louder than before.

And yet, he still continued to pound in and out of me, and he was giving it to me so good I couldn't imagine myself stopping this even if my boyfriend were to accidentally open the door of the room.

Moments later, it was finally over, and then Fred pulled out of me. When he did that, I noticed he was so tired, but that look in his eyes... It showed me that he was more than ready for round two, but I was far too tired for something like that, and thus I just collapsed on the bed.

I was huffing, but I had a huge smile on my face, and even though I knew this would never happen again between us, I knew that it changed something fundamental between us.

He propped his head on his hand, smiling. His smile was as devilish as before, and this time he looked even more stunning. Perhaps it was the gleam of sweat covering his body that was doing that, that was making me think that, but even if that were the case, it didn't change anything.

This was and would always be nothing more than a one-night stand, and he needed to get used to that.

"That was amazing, Madeine. You were amazing. I didn't think you were like that, and especially that you were so hungry and thirsty for me. Do you want to do this again next night?"

He asked me, and I wasn't surprised by his question. I was already expecting it, to be honest.

"I think that right now I just want to rest a little, then I want to put my clothes back on, clean myself up as best as possible, and then leave this place pretending that nothing of this happened. You are the president of The Burnt Rodents, but that still doesn't change anything, especially because James wouldn't hesitate before shooting you if it meant getting his revenge if he finds out about what happened here."

He shook his hand dismissively. "You don't need to worry about that. He's not going to learn anything about this, and I'm going to make sure of it." And after Fred promised that, he leaned over, kissing me on the lips, and it made me remember how much I was going to miss his lips on mine.

"I hope you're right about that," I said, closing my eyes as I felt his arm going around me. He was holding me tightly to him, and it was making me feel safe, protected, and warm.

I just could not sleep like this, and I really wasn't going to. I was only closing my eyes.

CHAPTER 6

Madeine

Thank God that James never found out anything about it. I didn't know if he knew, but ever since then, I had begun to feel something strange about my body. Some nausea. Something like that. Some pain in my stomach, and I was doing everything in my power to believe that it wasn't what I thought it was.

And ever since then, Fred had shown up more times when he was certain that James was nowhere close by. Every time that he had the opportunity, he came to me, his hands exploring my body, showing me how much he loved me – or maybe I was just imagining things.

He always said that he would never find true love, and I believed him. That was why I didn't want to think that anything was going on between us – at least, nothing more than him wanting to fuck me.

Nevertheless, that was far from my thoughts at the moment. I was beginning to grow suspicious. I was in my car, outside of the drug store, where I could find the pregnancy test I was looking for.

It was dark and raining. I could see and hear the rain pounding on the frame of the car, the windshield wipers moving left and right, and left and right again and again.

Was I making a mistake? Hell no! I wasn't making a mistake because I was doing the right thing. I needed to be certain about this, and there was only one way to do that, and it was by taking a pregnancy test.

I took a deep breath, opened the door of my car, and then headed to the drugstore without taking out my umbrella. Even the only desk attendant inside the store was looking at me with wide eyes. The water was drenching my clothes, and nobody would be subjecting themselves to this unless they were desperate about something.

I entered the store and started to look inside it for a pregnancy test box, and for some reason, I couldn't find it. I was probably so scared that I couldn't even spot the glowing, obvious sign that said where it had to be, right?

I didn't know, I thought, and then, when I felt a hand on my shoulder, I was even more spooked than before. It was none other than the clerk of the drug store, I realized, but then, after blinking again, I noticed that he was actually someone else.

Someone I knew well. Someone that shouldn't be here unless he was following me. *Unless he was stalking me.*

"Madeine, what are you doing here? And why arc you looking like this? You look like such a mess," he said, and after blinking again to make sure that I wasn't having a hallucination, I realized that he really was Fred.

He was wearing his leather jacket, jeans pants, the silver necklace around his neck, and rings on his fingers. Everything about him showed me that he was the president of the Burn Rodents, and also that... we shouldn't be seeing each other like this.

"Let's go somewhere where he can't hear us, where *nobody* can hear us," I said, taking him over to the other side of the drugstore, where we were so far from the attendant that he really couldn't hear us.

"What's going on?" Fred asked, his eyes narrowing. He knew something was up, and now that he knew that, he wasn't going to let go. He was going to keep prodding until he got the answer he was looking for.

I bit my bottom lip, turning around and noticing that right

behind me was what I was looking for here. A pregnancy test box and I felt relieved knowing that I had found it.

This was it. I was going to take the pregnancy test and it was going to show me that I wasn't pregnant and that all my fears were unfounded, even though the last part wasn't exactly true. I did have all the right and common symptoms for pregnancy, and I guessed that I just didn't want to admit that to myself.

"Wait here for me. I'm going to be back in a bit," I said, taking one of the pregnancy test boxes, going to the desk attendant, paying for it, and then stepping inside the bathroom. I was happy that this drugstore had a bathroom, I thought, closing the door of the stall behind me.

And I did what I needed to do, peeing so that the test had what it needed to work. I shook the test tube in my hand, making sure that I did everything right, and then the seconds passed, and the first and the second lines appeared, and… I felt more nervous than ever before in my life.

Even my boyfriend had begun to notice that something was off about me, and he had also begun to ask me questions about it, and so far, I had managed to navigate through them, but now that this was happening and I realized that I really was pregnant, I knew that all hell was going to break loose.

My life had just turned upside down, and I couldn't do anything about that.

I stepped out of the bathroom after putting my pants back on and noticing that Fred was standing outside of the drugstore, getting back on his motorcycle.

I knew that I was pregnant and that he was most likely the father, so I was livid that he was leaving without saying anything that could make me feel better. And now, after all the moments we went through together, I needed his support. I thought that he was a better man than this.

And he looked over his shoulder the moment that he picked up his motorcycle helmet. He was going to put it on when he realized that something was terribly wrong with me, and then he got off his motorcycle, coming with me to my car.

He knew I had something important to say to him and that here, in my car, we could talk about it without anyone hearing anything.

21

CHAPTER 7

Fred

I had no idea what was going on, but I knew it was serious. She was gripping my hand as though she planned on yanking it off me, which was a silly thought, but which also reflected how worried she was feeling, and me being me, I knew I had to do something about it.

If it was because of James, then he was going to suffer for it. I wouldn't let it slide.

"What's going on, Madeine? Why are you looking so worried? " I asked, hoping that she was going to give me a straight answer, but the seconds were passing and she wasn't saying anything. Not yet, anyway.

When I was going to say something else, she finally blurted out, "I'm pregnant, Fred, and I'm certain that you are the father."

The moment she said that it was like I had been struck by a meteor. She was pregnant and I was the father? What? It had been some months since we fucked, but I had put on a condom and she had also told me she was on birth control. Unless she had lied about it, which I didn't think she had.

"What? That doesn't make any sense. You said that you were on birth control, and I used a condom to make sure that something like this never happened."

"I don't know. I was beginning to feel some symptoms, like nausea and feeling tired all the time, and also these weird food cravings, and then I decided to come here to take the test, and it's showing positive," Madeine said, holding the box in front of me in her hand.

Madeine really was right about it. The box showed what it showed, highlighting to me the two, bright red lines, and that indeed, she was pregnant.

"I'm sure that you are mistaken about this. We were careful and not to mention that you have James. I'm sure that you two have sex from time to time, right?" I asked, taking my hand off of hers.

Shit. I didn't like where this was going. If she was pregnant, then she had to abort, in case the baby was really mine, but she was still James' old lady, and I was certain that chances were higher that he was the father and not me.

Madeine was out of her mind. She had to be imagining things.

I was looking through the windshield and ahead, admiring the rain pounding against the car. It was relatively calm here and outside, and seconds passed without her saying anything. I thought Madeine was going to cry, but she was stronger than that, and she was still staring at me as though she wanted to slap my face, and she would have all the right to do that.

And I noticed that her cheeks were flushing. Why? I asked myself, and then I noticed that she was already going to say something about that.

"We've never had sex. He's always so busy with other things, always going out at night, always getting piss drunk, and always leaving me alone. Why do you think that I started to feel something for you? Even though you are his best friend and the president of the Burnt Rodents, you are also the only man that has shown that you care about me – at least, a little bit more than he does."

I blinked twice, not believing her words. She just said to me that they'd never had sex, but that didn't make any sense. Whenever James talked about her, he always said how much he loved her, how much he cared about his old lady, and all the cliches. I was even getting tired of all that.

But then, I studied her eyes and I noticed that she wasn't kidding. She wasn't pulling my leg, and I could feel that thanks to the single tear that escaped her left eye and was now rolling down her cheek.

"You are... really serious about this?" I asked, my heart skipping a bit. What I had said about her aborting was... something that just came out of my mouth, but which I didn't really mean.

I just wasn't ready for this.

I wasn't ready for her to get pregnant, for the baby to be mine, and to become a father. I mean, just look at me. I was a biker. I killed people, robbed, liked traveling across the state on my motorcycle, seeing new people, new faces, and that sort of thing.

"Well, we have to take the DNA test just to make sure," I suggested and, for a moment, I thought she was going to argue against that, but then she took a deep breath, looking forward and through the windshield, watching the rain pelting the city.

"I don't like it, but you're right. We need to make sure that the baby is really yours too before we do anything, and until then... What do you suggest I tell James? The more he notices that my belly is growing bigger, he will start to ask questions even more incisive than the ones he has already been making, and it will be the end of my life."

She needs my support now more than ever. I put my hand on her cheek, caressing it. "I'm going to be here for you and no matter what happens, I know that you are going to get through it. Worst case scenario, you can convince James that the baby is his and that should be the end of all this."

And yes, there was something about it that I felt was wrong. Perhaps it was the fact that I didn't believe my words. If I was the father, I could feel a certain part of me that said I should accept that and start a new chapter in my life.

Well, I didn't know about any of that right now, but there was something I could do that was going to make her forget all of this, even if only momentarily.

And that was me kissing her.

CHAPTER 8

Madeine

Fred just kissed me. All of a sudden. And it looked like everything I needed. The moment that our lips touched, I felt something different. I felt all the rage, all the pain, all the sadness, and pretty much everything else washing out of me, and I also felt so much better I couldn't believe that I was letting this whole thing devour me from the inside out.

He slipped his tongue between my lips and we had a short tongue battle. It was short because even though I put up a fight, he was much the better kisser and also so much more dominant.

I felt his arms going around me and then his fingers under my shirt. Shit. Was this really happening? Did he want to fuck me in my car? I was certain that even though James didn't really care about me anymore, he would notice something different about the interior of it. The smell would be perceptible, and that was putting it mildly.

But now that he was already lifting my shirt, and then his fingers worked to unhook my bra, I couldn't do anything. What comforted me was knowing that it was dark around here, especially inside the car. Not even the clerk inside the drugstore was going to notice anything, and I knew that we could fuck without anyone ever finding out anything about this.

His lips were wet, hot, sweet, and just like the way that I remembered they were that first time we kissed. And he was such a good kisser that I couldn't believe that I missed his lips so much.

I felt his fingers unhooking my bra and then he took it off me, depositing it in the backseat. He broke our kiss, something that saddened me the moment it happened, and then he pulled his head back, his eyes assessing my body and scrutinizing every part of it.

"Holy shit, you're still so gorgeous. I don't know exactly what's going on in your mind, but you don't need to worry about anything. I'm going to be with you all the way through this," he promised me, and looking into his eyes, I knew that he wasn't kidding. He wasn't pulling my leg. He wasn't lying to me, and that was so much more than James ever did for me.

"Just kiss me again," I begged and he grinned, showing me his perfect teeth, something unusual when it came to bikers. He went to the dentist often, I could tell.

Then, I felt his lips crashing down on mine again, and I was breathless. And I just had to have more, and especially to do something I was unable to do when we first fucked. My fingers desperately looked for his belt, which I took off in a moment before he could do anything about it, and then he smiled again when he realized what was going on.

"It's like you're not even worried about the pregnancy anymore," he joked, his hands moving over my legs, massaging them, feeling every part, and then stopping when he was no more than a couple of moments from finding my pussy.

It was already wet for him, and I could imagine myself letting him fuck me again here, and in my car, the rain battering on the frame of the vehicle, and everything was like he had just said. I wasn't worried about being pregnant anymore. I could feel the rush of adrenaline and joy in my body, and it was addictive.

"Just shut up and kiss me again," I said, my fingers now lowering his pants and then his pair of boxer briefs. And then I dared to open my eyes and I found his cock, and for the first time I was seeing it, and it was as big as I'd thought.

He had shaved down there, too. I could also see his balls, his scrotum, and how low it hung. His nuts were big and appeared to be laden with his sperm. The sperm that most likely made the baby that was now in my belly, and the thought of finally wrapping my lips around it... It was making me feel goosebumps all over my body.

"I know I shouldn't be doing this, but fuck it. A bit too late to worry about that," I purred, pushing myself down and then enveloping my lips around his prick, and then I started to swirl my tongue around his cockhead, enjoying it, cherishing it, and worshiping it.

I had never had sex until that moment, and this was actually the first time that I was giving a man head, and the most striking thing about this moment was that he was enjoying it. After glancing up, I noticed the joy and lust in Fred's eyes, and then he put his hand on my head, dictating the pace that he wanted.

I didn't say anything, and there was nothing to be said anyway.

He tilted his head back, relaxing his body in the seat. He widened his legs slightly, giving me a little bit more space, and then I felt his fingers grabbing my hair slightly and certainly not to the point where he was hurting me.

"Jesus, Madeine. What you said before is making me think that this is the first time you are giving a blowjob, but the way that you are moving your tongue around it, feeling every part of my dick, is making me think that you have a lot of experience."

I didn't know anything about that, but I was happy that it was working and that he was enjoying it.

CHAPTER 9

Madeine

I was going to continue until he was cumming into my mouth, and I knew he wanted that, too. Fred didn't do anything other than dictating the pace he wanted with his hand, and my hands did everything they could to feel his body, his massive balls, and play with and tug them, and then I could feel how much he was enjoying this.

I could also feel that, as time passed, he was close to his climax, and I couldn't help but wonder what I would feel when his milk was filling my mouth. I couldn't wait for it.

His hand started to fumble with my breasts, and the feeling was so exhilarating that every time his fingers grazed over my nipples, goosebumps tickled my skin. I felt waves of pleasure traveling in it and I just wanted this moment to last forever.

Things were getting quite messy, too. I could feel the saliva making everything slippery, wet, and everything else that came with that. But it wasn't enough to stop me, and I just continued to bob up and down on his prick, enjoying every moment of this.

His cock was so warm.

My body was hot, and every time that I felt his fingers playing with my boobs, I felt like this would never end.

"Jesus, Madeine. You're going to make me come in your mouth in record time."

Did he even need to say that? I asked myself, realizing that there was no point to his words, but that was all so unimportant right now, too.

"I'm going to make you do so much more than that," I promised, mumbling, and I wasn't even sure if he was able to make out my words or not. What had come out of my mouth was just gibberish, given that my lips were more worried about pleasing his prick than anything else, and I was almost getting ahead of myself, too.

I knew that I loved his balls. I loved his scrotum, the texture on my fingers, his hand still clutching my hair, my head moving up and down, and then I noticed that he was finally on the verge of coming.

I knew that tomorrow morning I was probably going to wake up with a sore, hurt throat, but it didn't matter. What mattered was swallowing all of his sperm, something that I had always meant to do when we first fucked, but he had also never allowed me to do that, so I was making up for it.

"I'm going to come, Madeine. Last chance to pull back your head," he warned, but there was no point in doing that. I wasn't moving my head anywhere other than up and down along his massive prick.

And then, it finally happened. The eruption I was looking for. I felt him shooting rope after rope of his warm sperm in my mouth, and my throat worked to swallow all of them down, and it was as salty as I had thought. Creamy, delicious, and I couldn't have enough of it.

I didn't know that I could be so slutty, but by now it was all over and I had to clean myself up, especially so that James never noticed that something was wrong.

With a grunt, I pulled my head back, not wanting to do that, but having to do so anyway, especially because I needed to go back home. I looked into his eyes, and I saw a man that could be the father of my baby, but was I really reading that right?

I didn't know, but it didn't matter right now. I was tired. I knew that I was pregnant, and I had to work on how to break the news to my boyfriend. He was drunk so often, so I was going to use that to my advantage. I was going to say to him that we fucked when he was drunk and that now he couldn't remember anything because of that.

"Are you sure you're going to be okay?" He asked after putting his pants back on, cleaning himself up with some tissue paper, and then opening the door of the car.

He was acting so differently from his usual self right now. He was looking at me with care in his eyes, and I never thought that I would notice something like that from him.

I nodded. "Yeah, I should be okay. It's going to take me some time, but I'll eventually have to break the news to my boyfriend. I don't know how he'll take it, but I think that everything is going to be okay."

"I hope so. Either way, he looks at me as a figure of authority, so I know that he will never hurt you, and especially after I make sure that if he does something like that, I'll kill him."

I chuckled slightly and uncomfortably. I knew who I was dealing with and the kind of man Fred was.

He kissed me on my lips again.

"It's going to be okay. Regardless of what happens, I'm going to make sure that everything is going to be alright," he promised and I knew that it was a promise he would uphold no matter what happened.

"Thanks, but I really have to go now, and there's so much I have to think about," I said and then he nodded, closing the door of the car. I looked ahead, found the road, turned on the engine of the car, and then I started to drive toward my house.

I still had no idea how I was going to break the news to my boyfriend, but it still needed to be done, and nothing could change that.

CHAPTER 10

Madeine

"**I**'m sorry?" He asked me, putting his hand on his chest and looking threatening. He loomed in front of me, and for a moment I thought he was going to hit me, which would be a first between us.

Our relationship was going through a lot of turbulence right now, but I never thought that things were so bad that he would ever consider hitting me. Thankfully, it appeared that he was only pissed off.

After all, it had been months, and my belly had grown bigger, and he had finally realized that something was up with me. I couldn't hide my secret any longer, and I had to tell him the truth.

I had been doing the prenatal procedures and everything appeared to be fine, though it was also all in the initial stages. The doctor hadn't even checked yet if my baby was a girl, a boy, or even if I had more than one baby in my belly.

Given how huge my belly had grown, it was possible that it was more than one baby, and if that was the case, my life would get worse – worse than it already was, I thought.

"I'm sorry. I didn't know what to do. One moment everything was fine with me, then I started to feel some symptoms, and then today I finally mustered up enough courage to take the pregnancy test, and it's positive," I said, holding up the pregnancy test tube in my hand, and he snatched it from me.

His eyes checked it for a brief second and then he tossed the tube over his head, and I watched it as it hit the wall and then fell down on the floor. What he just did spoke more about his reaction than all of his previous words combined, and that hit me like a runaway train.

"You... didn't know what to do? Jesus, Madeine. You should have told me before that you were feeling the symptoms and you should have taken the pregnancy test way before today so that we knew the truth and we had more time to prepare." He took a deep breath, running his hand over his face. "You know how poor we are. You know what we are going through, and you know that we can't have a baby. I don't even have enough money for our food and I'm sorry, but that's exactly the way things are, and I would love to have a baby and be a father, but things don't work like that, and especially not for me."

I was frozen where I was, trying to make sense of his words. He just told me that we couldn't even keep the baby fed, and I couldn't have that. I couldn't accept it.

"So, you're just going to let the baby die?" I asked and, for a moment, there was no response. He had dropped his body onto the couch, his arms spread over the armrests, and he was looking out the window that faced the road in front of the house without showing any emotion.

I knew that James was thinking, and I knew what he was going to do before he even did.

He just stood up in a blink, rushing to the door. I went after him, put my hand on his shoulder, and I was going to stop him, but then I realized how pointless it all was.

"What are you going to do?" I asked, hoping that he was going to change his mind, but knowing how stubborn he was, I knew I couldn't do that.

Not to mention that he had just turned his head around to glare at me with threatening eyes, and for a moment I had really thought that he was going to hit me.

"Somewhere where I can think," he said, slamming the door shut behind him and then storming out of the house, leaving me completely alone.

I was stuck where I was, unable to think, unable to move, and then when I could finally move, I headed over to the couch, sitting where he had been sitting, but in my case, it was more like I just let my body fall onto it.

I didn't know what to do and then I soon found myself crying and hiding my face in my hands.

After some minutes of crying, I finally decided to do something I thought I would never do. I picked up my phone from the pocket in my pants, looked for Fred's contact number, and then dialed it.

The connection kept calling him and I thought he wouldn't pick up, but then he did, and when he heard my muffled sobs and crying, he asked, sounding alarmed, "Madeine? What's going on? Why are you crying? If it's because of that asshole, then I'm going to kill him, best friend or not. I'm going to feed him to my dogs."

I chuckled, suddenly feeling that some of the weight was lifting off my shoulders.

"Y-yes, it was because of him. I mean, it is because of him that I'm crying, and you don't need to do anything."

"What did he say?" He asked, his tone threatening.

"He said that we aren't going to have enough money to support the baby, and now I'm fearing that he or she will probably die because we don't have enough money for food."

"That's bullshit! He's spending everything on beer and you know it. I need to have a long, deep talk with him, and then I'll tell him everything as it is, and if he doesn't change, you are mine."

For a moment, I didn't even know what to say. I knew that Fred was going to be overprotective, as he always was, but I never thought that he would just straight up say that he was going to take me from my boyfriend. That was escalating things, and I was kind of afraid of it.

And yet, it was kind of good.

CHAPTER 11

Fred

The moment when I found out that she was crying in the middle of the night, I had to do something. That was why the first thing I did was to hop onto my motorcycle, turn on the engine, and then head over to her house as quickly as possible.

The tires screeched to a halt and I hopped off the motorcycle right away, throwing open the door of her house. She was seated on the couch, and the moment when I noticed the tear lines on her face, I knew that she needed my support, and even though I didn't look at her as my girlfriend, I was going to do everything in my power so that she felt more comfortable.

"Jesus, Madeine. You are stronger than this. He shouldn't have just abandoned you the way he did. He's my friend and also my second-in-command, so I'll have a long, serious talk with him and I'll put him back in his place. That I promise you."

She chuckled when I sat by her side, and then she threw her arms around me. It had been a couple more months since we last saw each other, and even though her belly was bigger now, she was still so stunning that the first thing that came into my mind was how much I wanted to fuck her.

I had heard stories that women usually felt a lot more sex drive when they were pregnant, and thus I found myself thinking about that, and how right it was.

Now that she could feel my body against hers, she was already a lot better and crying less.

"I'm not strong, or at least, not as strong as I had thought," she confessed, her eyes going up and down and checking me out from bottom to top. The moment when she did that, I knew that look in her eyes, and I knew what she wanted.

I wanted the same. My cock was hard, and she was looking so tempting.

"Did the doctor ever tell you if it's okay for you to have sex when you are this pregnant?" I asked, my fingers brushing under her shirt and feeling the bump. It was my baby.

It was either my baby boy or my baby girl, and I couldn't help but wonder how they would look when they were a little older, and when they were playing football with me, and when they were calling me daddy, and... There were so many other things that were beginning to sprout up in my mind.

What was even going on with me? I asked myself. Why were these thoughts beginning to sprout up in my mind all of a sudden? I didn't know, but I still took a deep breath in, and I waited for her answer.

"I haven't actually been seeing the doctor often about the baby. At least, not as often as I should be," she confessed and I couldn't help but feel some irritation in my heart.

"We need to do something about that. It's not okay."

"I don't have much more money for the pre-natal."

"I'm going to get you money. I'm going to give you as much money as you need, and we are going to pay for all the prenatal procedures, and everything is going to be fine because I'm saying so. James doesn't want to be the father that he should be, and even though that's not fine, we're going to deal with it. I can't go out right now and set him straight, but that can wait. Your happiness is more important than that."

"Thank you, Fred. I knew I could count on you," she said, brushing her lips against mine, and then I couldn't stop myself before kissing her. It felt so right to be kissing her, especially now that her sex drive appeared to be burning hotter, her body needing more of me.

We had at least taken the DNA test, and I knew that I was the father. The only problem was that we still didn't know if it was a baby boy or baby girl, or if it was more than one baby, but that hardly mattered right now.

What mattered was making sure that Madeine was smiling, and she was doing that right now.

I pushed her until she was lying down on the couch, and then I did something I was sure she didn't think I was going to, picking her up in my arms.

She gasped, chuckling. When she realized what I was about to do and when she noticed my hard-on, she couldn't help but ask, "Wait, what do you think you're doing? I have no idea where James went and he may come back soon. We can't do it here."

I smiled devilishly. "Do I look like I care about that?" I replied, kicking open the door of her bedroom, and then the next thought that crossed my mind was that I was going to fuck her again, for the third time in a couple of months, and in her own bedroom no less, which she shared with her boyfriend.

I knew she was thinking the same thing, which was why she was looking at me with such wide eyes. "But we really shouldn't, and I don't want to hurt the baby."

"Don't worry. I'm going to be careful," I promised, and it was difficult for me to wipe the smile off my face. It was dirty, naughty, and when I finally put her down on the bed, I wasn't even thinking about that.

The only thing I was thinking about was stripping the clothes off my body right away, which I was doing. Pregnant or not, I was going to fuck Madeine until she was crying out my name, especially because I knew it was the best way to keep that smile on her face. It was radiant, and I couldn't stop looking at it.

We had fought so many times before, but now she was nothing more than my prey, though I was still going to make sure that everything was going to be alright with her.

So much so that I didn't hold anything back when I dropped my body where she was, crashing our lips together.

Gosh, I would never get enough of the taste of her sweet lips.

CHAPTER 12

Madeine

I really had no idea what I was doing, but it was good. I could feel his fingers all over my body, pinching my nipples, fumbling with my breasts, and it was all only the beginning. His lips were dangerously close to mine, and I wondered if he was going to kiss me again, but that smile on his face... It showed me that he wasn't even thinking about doing that. What he was thinking about was actually teasing me a little more, something that he was so good at doing.

"We really shouldn't be doing this," I tried to say, but then he clamped his hand on my mouth, showing me how pointless my plea was.

"You know you want it, and there is no point in delaying the inevitable anyway," he said, and I couldn't help but wonder what exactly was going on in his mind. Sometimes, Fred said the weirdest of things, but other times he was on point, and right now... I supposed that nothing of that mattered.

He ripped off my shirt, unhooked my bra, removed it, and now I was entirely exposed. He had been doing his dirty, naughty things before with his hands under my clothes, but now not anymore, and knowing that was showing me how hungry he was.

I could feel his hot breath on my face.

I could feel his fingers pinching my nipples again.

I could feel his hands roaming over my entire body, and that wasn't even the beginning of it. Moments later, he kissed me again, and some seconds after that, I felt him lowering my pants, and I couldn't do anything to stop him, not that I was even trying to, anyway.

When he took off my pants, I wrapped my legs around his body, and I made sure that he wasn't going to go anywhere. He was naked from top to bottom, and it was such a delight to see his body naked and exposed, just like I was. I could see each and every one of his tattoos, and they were even more threatening than my boyfriend's, something I never thought possible until now.

I couldn't help but gasp, looking down and noticing that his immense, meaty cock was pointed right to my pussy, which was dripping wet. I couldn't help but wonder how I was going to manage this, and especially given that I was a couple of months pregnant already.

His fingers roamed over my belly and then he put himself right in front of my pussy, his tongue flicking out.

"And there are so many amazing things I want to do to you, and it all starts now," he said, flicking his tongue over my clit, rubbing on it, driving me wild, and then, as if to show me that it wasn't enough, he decided to do something else. Something that was even more threatening, and which I knew was going to send ripples of pleasure all through my body.

He slid his tongue inside my pussy.

He looked up and then said, "It's such a pity that, this whole time, James hasn't been doing much with you. I'm thinking that, deep down, he knows that I'm the one that owns you. He knows you are my property, and when the time is right, I'm going to show him that he doesn't need to worry about anything. I'm the one that's going to make you happy."

His dirty talk was pushing all the right buttons in me, and I couldn't help but clamp my legs tighter around his body. "You really don't want me to go anywhere, right?" He asked and all I could do was nod.

This whole time, he continued to run his tongue over my pussy, focusing on my bundle of nerves, slipping it inside my entrance every so often, and sometimes even using his fingers, playing with my pussy folds. And he was making me so wet I just couldn't believe that it was all happening like this.

I was so ready for when he penetrated me, and I was certain he was thinking about doing that as well. With a grunt, Fred pulled back, and he gave me a good, long look, scrutinizing every part of me, and then he put my legs over his shoulders and went inside of me without showing a hint of mercy or any cue that he could be stopped.

I closed my eyes as I said, "Gosh, you are so big. I don't know how I was able to fit you inside of me the first time."

"Don't worry. If there's something I learned about you, it's that you can accommodate any man inside of you, even though, from this moment onward, you are mine only, and you can only have sex with me. I'm going to tell James everything so that he knows that this is happening."

I didn't even know how he was going to go about that, but it felt good. It felt right to have a man willing to do so much for me, even though for the time being, it was just for the sex, which I loved.

He rolled his hips and I matched him thrust for thrust, pounding my body against his, and this time, since he knew that I couldn't get pregnant again, he decided to do this without using a condom. It was hot as fuck, and everything I wanted.

"Cum with me, Madeine. Cream all over my cock. Show me how much you want me, and show me that you are my property," he said, and I couldn't hold it back any longer. I cried out his name so loud that I knew the neighbors must have heard it, and yet I didn't care about it, or about the possible consequences, and especially if the neighbors would tell James about what they heard.

When he was finished, I looked into his eyes and I could see someone that could be so much more to me.

I didn't know what the future held in store for me, but I had a chance and I would never squander it.

More and more, Fred was showing me that there was

something under his external personality that showed me he could be more. Maybe he really could be the father of my baby, or babies.

CHAPTER 13

Fred

"What the hell did you just say?" James yelled, trying to punch me, but the swing of his arm was too slow, and I was able to dunk and avoid his attempt without even fearing – not even once – that he could hit me. He was fucked up by the fact that he now knew I was fucking his old lady, and he couldn't do anything about it.

We were standing in this open region between a couple of houses. There was a large, bright spotlight shining on us, making this all look like it was a big fight. And indeed, it was. Between us. James was my friend. Had been, I corrected myself. No point in thinking that there was still anything significant going on between us in terms of that, especially after finding out about all the things that he was doing to his own girlfriend.

"You are an asshole. Madeine needs someone better, and I think that that person is me," I taunted, opening my arms out wide and hoping that he was going to take the bait, but he didn't. He tried kicking me instead, which didn't work in his favor at all. I blocked it and then I hit him with my knee, and it was loud and strong enough for me to feel how much it hurt him.

"She's not yours!" He barked, trying to go and hit me again, but then he stumbled and lost his balance, falling to one knee. James was huffing, and I could see the blood coming out of his nose. He really thought that everything was going to be just fine and dandy between his girlfriend and him, but he didn't know, this whole time, that I was the father of the baby.

Or babies, I corrected myself. After a couple more tests and waiting a bit longer, we found out that Madeine was pregnant with twins.

"She's mine, and there is nothing you can do about it," I said, punching his face and then seeing blood coming out of his mouth and nose. He thought he was so different.

James thought he was better than me, and I knew that because he'd always been like that. Like this. He would never change.

He was still with one knee on the floor and he had all the reasons to kill me, but none of them were going to be sufficient. After all, I was the one on top. Even though I had never thought that a moment like this would come, now that it was happening, it was pumping me up.

It was making me think I could do anything and everything and come out of it unscathed.

Another punch.

And then another.

And then one more, for good measure, and before long, his entire body fell on the ground. The spotlight shone on it, showing how hurt and beaten-up he looked right now, and it was still not sufficient to make me stop. If anything, I was going to keep on going.

With that thought in mind, I straddled him, putting myself on top of him and fisting my hands. I was going to do it. I was going to kill my former best friend, and it couldn't be stopped anymore.

My heart was pumping blood a lot faster and harder than before, and I couldn't stop myself.

Another punch on his face.

And then another.

And then one more.

Until I could see teeth flying out of his mouth, and that wasn't even the beginning of this. I kept on punching his face for what felt like an eternity, then I only stopped when I heard a shriek behind me. My chest was huffing, and I could feel the sweat forming on my forehead.

Someone was seeing this. Someone was watching me do this, and I had to do something about it. I didn't think this through, but now that it was obvious that someone was going to tell everyone about this, I needed to do something about it.

With that thought in mind, I turned my head around slowly until I found the person that was standing no more than a couple of feet from me. She was none other than Madeine, and I couldn't wrap my head around her being here.

When did she show up? What was she doing here? She should be home, looking after herself, taking care of herself, doing everything possible so that everything was okay with our babies.

But now, she was here, seeing this horrible, gut-wrenching, and uncontrollable part of me, and I was beginning to think I just fucked something up. Something that couldn't be fixed easily.

"You are a monster," she said, speeding over to me. I thought that she was going to throw her arms around me and tell me over and over again that she didn't mean what she said, but that wasn't what happened.

She went over to her former boyfriend. The man that never really cared about her. She went down on her knees and cried over him, making me realize how unbelievable this whole thing was.

I did all of this for her.

She had no idea what James had been spouting out recently about her and what he was going to do to her and me.

James thought he was bigger than me, more important, that he controlled more of my men and could be a threat, but he was just stupid, weak, and I just showed him that.

By killing him.

CHAPTER 14

Madeine

He wiped the blood off the knuckles of his hands, looking at me as though he didn't care about this at all. I had no idea what he was thinking, but at least he wasn't smiling or looking like his usual, overconfident self.

If anything, something was hurting him right now, and that might just be my reaction to this.

I didn't know that he had gone into a fight with my former boyfriend, if I could even still call him that. I couldn't even stand to look at his face. Fred had beaten it into an unrecognizable pulp, only meat, teeth, his eyes sunken in, his nose turned to the other side, the nostrils completely closed, and no part of his body was even moving.

He wasn't even breathing. I'd even checked for his pulse, but there was nothing. I then put my ear over his chest, and I couldn't hear anything. He wasn't breathing. His heart wasn't beating, and all of that could only mean one thing.

He was really dead, and it meant that I couldn't look at the man standing behind me with the same eyes anymore. He had just killed my boyfriend, and that was something I could never forgive or forget.

"Why are you crying so much for a piece of shit like him?" Fred asked, looking incredulous and crossing his arms over his chest. I supposed it was a good thing that it appeared that this place was so isolated that there was no chance that anyone would eventually stumble over here while we were still here.

I just didn't want the police or anyone to come over here and find us like this.

"You just killed James. I'll never forgive you," I promised, gritting my teeth.

"Oh, come on. You've got to be kidding me. This whole time, you were moaning about him, telling me that you didn't like him at all, and you even told me one night that you didn't want anything else to do with him, and also that he was making your whole life miserable."

"That doesn't have anything to do with this. You've got no idea what you are doing, what you're saying, and everything you're telling me right now is making me feel so disgusted at you. I fucking hate you!" I yelled, standing up in a blink, and tipping up my chin.

What did he think was going to happen when he did this? I did once fear that they were going to have a fight, but I didn't think that Fred was capable of doing this.

After all, James had been his best friend and his second-in-command. They had gone through so much, and now this… This was happening.

I couldn't believe any of this. Couldn't wrap my head around it.

I wanted to cry even more than I already was, and I couldn't hold it back any longer. Fred was still looking at me with his nose tipped up, staring down at me as though nothing of this mattered, and it was then that it dawned on me. He really saw me as nothing more than his property and that would never change.

I felt his hand on my shoulder.

I knew he wanted to tell me something, perhaps say something that would change my mind about this, but it was already too late, and I was already leaving this place anyway.

"Madeine, stop crying. You look like a fool right now, and the only thing this is doing is eating you from the inside out." He took a deep breath, still keeping his hand on my shoulder. "Let's go home. I'll call my guys to put him in a bag and then get rid of the body. They will understand what happened here."

"No!" I yelled, reopening my eyes quickly and then staring at him with questioning, frightened pupils. "You shouldn't do anything. I don't want you anywhere near me again, and I just want you gone from my life. That's everything I want right now," I yelled, taking off from there and then finding my car.

I threw open the door and locked it at the same moment that I noticed him banging his fist on the window. I shrieked. I thought he was going to start to pound on the window so hard that it would break, but it didn't go that far. Fred was a monster, but he would never hurt me.

When Fred realized that he wasn't going to change anything by being violent toward me, he took some steps away from the vehicle. I turned on the engine and just as I was driving away from there, he yelled, "I know that this doesn't end here, Madeine. You didn't even give me enough time to explain myself, and maybe one day you will. And when that happens, you will finally understand that I did the right thing."

I had no idea what he was thinking he was going to accomplish by saying something like that, but it wasn't working so far. He wasn't stopping my crying. In fact, he was only making it worse. I was crying and sobbing even more than before, especially after realizing that I was partially to blame for all of this.

After all, Fred wouldn't have done anything and it all would have remained the same if I hadn't gotten involved with him. If only I had stopped his advances on me before it was too late. If only I had established from the very beginning that we shouldn't do anything stupid. Not even that first kiss.

If that all had happened, then nothing of this would be happening, and it would all be better.

Not great. It wouldn't all be perfect, but it would be better than this.

CHAPTER 15

Madeine

I was in the kitchen, looking out the window and wondering what had happened. It had been some weeks, perhaps even months since that incident. Incident? It was a crime what he did. I would never forget it. Just thinking about it now, my hand was trembling. I couldn't stop it, and it was getting worse.

It was like it was happening now again. It was like I was standing a couple of feet away from them, watching it all happen in front of me. I didn't know why I hadn't been stronger.

I didn't know why I didn't try to stop it before it was too late.

Perhaps there was – had been – a part of me that wanted it to continue. Perhaps I wanted to see James dead, but I didn't think that was it.

Right now, everything was so quiet around me that I felt isolated. I felt like nothing could reach me here, and I felt at home. I felt my hands moving over my belly, reminding me that I was pregnant with twins. I'd always thought that something like this would never happen to me.

I didn't think I was ready to build a family, but here it was, it was happening, and there was nothing I could do about it.

My hand was holding a glass. I took sips from it every so often. It was gin. The taste was good, but it used to taste better. I didn't know if I was just imagining things, but that was my perception of it at the moment.

The taste used to be better, and I shouldn't be doing this. I shouldn't be drinking, especially not now that I was pregnant. In the end, I didn't have enough money to finish all the prenatal procedures. I did learn something important about my babies, though, and it was the fact that they were both boys. Little, cute baby boys. I had a scan of them, and they looked so cute that I just wanted to pinch their cheeks when they were finally out of me.

I put the glass down on the counter in the kitchen, turned around slowly, and was going to make my way to my bedroom when I felt a sharp pain in my belly. It wasn't the first time I felt a pain in my belly and I knew it wouldn't be the last.

Not to mention that I was getting used to the sudden pangs of pain, anyway. I should be, especially because I was almost 9 months pregnant.

And yet, this time it also felt different, and I began to feel some wetness between my legs, something that was starting all the alarm bells in my mind. Another pang of pain shot from my stomach, and now I knew that I should be more worried about what was going on here.

I felt lonely. I knew that nobody would come here after ditching Fred and yelling at him that he should never come here to look for me. I thought that he was bolder than that, but in the end, he respected my choice, and never came here looking for me, or in the usual places where I went to.

I had some people. Family members. Friends. Acquaintances. They could help me, but they also couldn't. I couldn't rely on them for more than bringing me food so that I didn't die.

That was why I decided not to call them, even though I realized it was something stupid.

I took another step forward and I tried to take another, and then I lost my balance, falling over on the floor. I managed to turn my body to the side just in time before hitting my stomach on the tiles, something that I would never have forgiven myself for if it had happened.

I grunted, gritting my teeth. I felt so much pain in my body that I couldn't believe it. I had to do something. Someone had to show up and take me to the hospital. Even though I didn't want to believe it, I knew that it was happening.

I was going into labor. I should have really chosen to have a cesarean delivery. That was what I should've done, but now it was too late, and I knew that my twins were coming.

I was desperate. I was looking at the door to the living room and I knew that nobody was going to come through it. Not in time, anyway. Not until it was too late and blood was coming out of my mouth and I and my babies were dead.

But then, I heard a motorcycle pulling over, and I knew that it had to be no one other than Fred. I knew that because I had heard his motorcycle engine so many times that my mind was attuned to it, and it just made sense that he was the one that was going to save me now, even though I hated him so much that I didn't even want to see his face again.

Moments later, he was right by my side, his eyes filled with worry.

"Oh Jesus, Madeine. I thought I was just imagining things, but it really is true, isn't it? I thought I was hallucinating. But, looking at you now, I realize that my gut feeling was right. You need to go to the hospital. Our babies are coming tonight!"

He was right about that, and part of me was happy that he was here, but I didn't show that.

"Just take me to the hospital. I have no idea how I'll pay all the bills, but I'll figure something out, and then you will never come back. I don't want to see your face ever again, especially after what you did to James."

Fred didn't say anything, and he couldn't just put me on his motorcycle to take me to the hospital. In light of that, he decided to put me in my car, in the passenger seat.

He sat down behind the steering wheel, turned on the engine, and then he drove off to the hospital. And I closed my eyes because I knew that, in the next couple of hours, I was going to be with my baby twins in my arms.

I knew that for certain because despite all the things that turned Fred into a monster, he was still reliable. He was going to take me there, make sure that everything was paid for, even if that meant that he was going to empty his bank account.

I should be okay.

CHAPTER 16

Fred

I knew I fucked it up. I fucked it all up and now she hated me more than anyone, even though she couldn't think that. She couldn't think that because she was holding both babies in her arms after the delivery. The birth went okay.

I couldn't believe it. I could scarcely believe it. After so many hours, so much pain, so much grunting, so much screaming, and so much everything else, she finally had my babies, and she was looking at them with a gleam of hope in her eyes.

Hope that everything was going to be better.

In the meantime, I was also hoping for the same, but this was also unfamiliar territory to me. I didn't know where I was stepping on. On one hand, I loved her – that was something I learned about me in the months when we didn't speak at all and after killing James – and on the other hand, she didn't like me anymore.

That she liked me? It was more like she hated me. She hated me with everything she had, and I couldn't fight against that. I felt powerless, especially now that I was just standing here by her hospital bed, wondering what I should be doing.

I never thought I would be a father and much less that the thought would grow on me. I loved it. I could imagine myself taking care of these cute baby boys. Playing with them. Teaching them things. Taking them to school, and that sort of thing. And even teaching them how to ride their first motorcycles.

It would be great, really.

And yet, I knew that it would never happen, especially because Madeine didn't want anything to do with me anymore. She made that known to me months ago and then again when I took her to the hospital.

At the time, I had a gut feeling that she needed me and that something terrible was happening to her. I had been right about it, but at the moment, nothing of that seemed to matter anymore.

She had my babies in her arms, but that was about it. This was the end of it all. I had paid for all the hospital bills, and I made sure that she was going to have everything, even though that meant I had to empty my bank account, and now I didn't even have any more money to keep the Burnt Rodents afloat, which meant that it was going to end.

My buddies would never forgive me for that, and I was already bracing for the backlash.

I turned around slowly after saying or rather mumbling something that not even I understood. I was unable to make out the words. I started to the door and when I put my hand on the doorknob, she said, "Fred, don't go. I want you here with me and with the babies. I know that you are thinking that you shouldn't be here, and perhaps you really shouldn't be, but I think that this might be a new beginning for us."

She took a deep breath and then she added, "It doesn't mean that I forgive you, but it's better than nothing, and it's better that you just leave me here alone. I need you. You are the father of our babies, and I need you so much."

I turned around slowly, my heart skipping beats. I couldn't believe what she had just said. Madeine said she needed me, she said she needed me for the babies and also for her, and I couldn't help but feel some wetness prickling on the sides of my eyes.

I went to her and didn't even know what to say. I felt like whatever I said, it would be gibberish and I would be mumbling, but still, I was happy. I was so happy that I wasn't able to hide the smile that crept up my face.

"Madeine, are you really sure about this? What happened between me and James... I know you would never forget it, but I also want to say that there's something about him you need to know."

She took a deep breath and then shook her head. "I know about it. I know all about it and what he was planning to do to me. My father told me everything, and I couldn't believe him when he said it, but now I know it was all true and I knew you were in the right to have that fight against him. I still don't think that you should have killed him, but what happened, happened, and I just want to make sure that this is a new beginning for us."

And then, there was a moment of silence, and I knew that Madeine was pondering her next words. I didn't know what she was going to say, but I knew it was going to be impactful, that it was going to shake me to the core.

"And I want you to stop being a biker. I want you to drop this whole thing, come and live with me somewhere else, where we could start a new life, where everything could be better than it is here. Can you do that for me? Can you come with me? Can you come with me and the babies?"

I took a deep breath in. That was a big decision for me, and I didn't know if I was ready for it.

FRED'S EPILOGUE

It was the most difficult decision of my life, especially because the Burnt Rodents had always been everything to me. I grew up with them. They were the ones that pretty much raised me, and I could never forget that. Not to mention that Harry, a.k.a. the 'Punisher' would never forgive me. He trusted the biker club to me, and he thought I was going to make it soar to higher levels, but that was all in the past now, and I couldn't change it.

I took her hand. We were still in the hospital and she was still on the hospital bed with the babies in her arms. Madeine was looking at me with such kind eyes, and after looking at the babies again, glancing at them, I knew that I had just one decision that could be made.

It was like she was cornering me against a wall, just like I had done to her so many times in the past.

"It's a big decision for me. You know that I'm not going to make it lightly," I said and she nodded. Of course Madeine knew that it was a big decision for me, and even though she couldn't change it, she was confident that I was going to pick the one she wanted.

"I'm going to be with you and we are going to start anew somewhere else," I said and I could see the smile appearing on her face. It was brighter than ever. Perhaps that was just thanks to the sunlight shining through the window and onto her face, but I knew that it was more than that. It was also thanks to how my mind was seeing this right now.

It really was a new beginning, wasn't it? This was the morning after the birth of our babies. After so many hours where I thought everything was going to go wrong…

The birds were chirping in the trees, the grass was greener than ever, and there was even a small stream behind the trees, something that I hadn't noticed until now.

"I knew you were going to make the right decision. I knew that you were going to support me no matter what," she said and I could feel the truth behind her words in her voice.

"Well, I'm happy that I'm going to be with Gary and Matthew," I said, hoping that I could spend some more hours with my babies. And just when I was thinking that was going to happen, the nurse came bursting through the door. Did nobody ever tell her that it was educated to knock before coming inside?

I shook my head, but it was obvious that she didn't even notice that. She was a fat, cocky woman in her thirties. Even though I didn't know her well, it was obvious that she wasn't the kind of person that would fear me just because I was a biker.

She had her hands on her waist, looking determinedly at me. "I think that I've given you enough time with the babies. They now need to be taken to the nursery, where they are going to be treated well and we are going to make sure that they have everything."

"What?" I asked, sounding incredulous. Of course I was going to be sounding like that. I hadn't been with my babies for more than a couple minutes, and I couldn't believe that she was already taking them from me.

She glanced at me, her eyes flicking up and down. She looked at me with some disdain in her eyes, and it was pretty obvious that she wasn't going to do anything I wanted just because I wanted it.

She flicked her finger up and down. "I think it's about time you understood that I'm the one running things here, and also the doctor told me that your babies really need to be taken to the nursery first, and that's the end of this little argument you want to start with me."

Just glancing at her eyes, I knew she was determined to do that, and I felt powerless against her, especially because I didn't want to cause any more trouble than I already had. Either way, spending some time alone with my old lady wasn't a bad thing at all, and I was already looking forward to it.

Old lady? I asked, noticing how wrong that was. She wasn't my old lady anymore. I didn't know what she was to me anymore, but she was still the mother of our babies, and that meant something.

"It's fine. You can take them," Madeine said and the tone of her voice told me everything I needed to know. If she was fine with the babies being taken away from her, then I was okay with that, though only partially.

"I know you were going to see reason," the cocky, joyful nurse said, putting the babies in her arms and then leaving the room, and leaving me completely alone with Madeine.

She chuckled. She looked so cute doing that and seeing that, I had to pull the chair closer to the hospital bed, sit on it, and then I took her hand. Madeine gazed into my eyes and she knew there was something important I needed to say. Something I was thinking about, but which I never thought would come to fruition. I never thought I would muster up enough courage to say it to her.

My throat was dry, and I was certain she was going to say no. Madeine was going to say that she didn't want to have something so deep, so strong with me, and there would be nothing I would be able to do about it.

MADEINE'S EPILOGUE

"**Y**ou said that we were going to live together in a different place. Does that mean what I think it means? Am I going to look stupid assuming something I think might be true, but which doesn't exist at all?" Fred asked, interlacing his fingers in his lap.

I had a suspicion about what he was going to ask me, and I didn't know if I was going to be right about it or not.

Still, this moment resonated with me, and I couldn't stop it anymore.

"I did say that, and I meant it. I want to live the rest of my life with you."

His Adam's apple bobbed up and down. It was the first time that he looked like that, and I didn't know how to react to it. I never thought that he would ever end his motorcycle club career, much less that he would ever be okay with that just because he was with me now.

"I want to marry you, Madeine. I know that there are still so many things between us that need to be resolved, but if there is something I know right now about this, it's that I want to marry you."

I took a deep breath in, but eventually, I realized that my mind was already made up about it. Fred wanted to marry me, and now that I had my babies with me, Gary and Matthew, and the sunlight was so bright outside, shining through the window, and everything felt so right, I knew that I couldn't say no.

"I want to marry you too, Fred," I said, taking his hand in mine and then kissing him. His lips were passionate, and as the seconds passed, I realized that he couldn't stop kissing me.

It was like he was telling me that if we ever did that, the first thing he would think was that we were already breaking up, which was ridiculous.

We ended the kiss and then he pulled his head back slightly, gazing into my eyes and regarding me with slight curiosity.

"I don't know how many times I've said this, but I love you so much. You are the only woman that I want to spend the rest of my life with," Fred confessed, and I knew he was truthful about that.

It didn't matter that we all thought that this moment would never come. Fred was making it happen, and now we were promising each other that we were going to get married.

"And I don't even know how it's going to happen, and even though I don't have enough money for it – at least, not right now – I'm going to make sure that when the time comes, I will have enough and I'll make the wedding the most beautiful there has ever been."

I didn't know he could be so romantic sometimes, but it filled my heart with joy that he was saying those words, and the more I looked into his eyes, the more I knew that he wasn't lying about it. He wasn't trying to fool me into thinking that he wasn't being serious about this.

He was, and it was everything I wanted.

I closed the door of the room. It was where our babies were. They were in separate cribs. The last thing I wanted was them starting a fight. They could be quite over-competitive sometimes.

They were twin brothers, and they looked so alike most of the time I didn't know who was who, which meant that I had to put two little pins on their onesies to make sure I didn't get confused.

His hand was on my shoulder. I looked behind my back, finding my husband. Thinking that he was my husband just felt so right, and I just couldn't imagine myself living a different life.

Despite all the problems we went through, everything worked out in the end, didn't it?

As for Fred killing James… I would never forget it, but I had kind of forgiven him for it, and we didn't talk about that anymore, anyway. It was in the past, just like our life in that city was. Everything about that city, that still connected us to it, was in the past, and I would never have it any differently.

He cupped my cheeks with his hands, kissing me. Fred now worked as a nightclub bouncer. It was much better than him building another motorcycle club, something I was certain that had crossed his mind several times before he dumped the idea altogether.

Relief washed over me just thinking about that. He shouldn't even have thought it was something feasible, that he could make happen without destroying our relationship.

We ended the kiss, and I walked with him to our bedroom. It wasn't far from the babies' room because we wanted to make sure that we would always hear everything in case we needed to. Not to mention that I was always kind of paranoid about them. They were my babies and I just wanted to make sure that everything was always going to be okay with them.

Fred could see the worry in my eyes. "Don't worry about the babies. Gary and Matthew are going to be okay. You don't need to wake up every 30 minutes and go and check on them. I know that they are going to be fine and that you can sleep for a couple of hours. You have heavy bags under your eyes, so I know how much your mind and body need a good night's sleep."

"I know," I said, opening a half smile. I really knew he was right, but it was always so difficult for me not to be overly worried about the babies, and I couldn't change that. "But it's always so difficult for me not to be so worried about them."

"Well, there's something we can do about that right now, and I know that it's going to bring a huge smile to your face."

He opened the door to our bedroom, and I couldn't help but look down, finding his big, massive cock under his pants.

And in light of that, all I could do was say, "Then, what are you

waiting for?”
He chuckled.
“I just knew you were going to say that…”
My love.
My life.
The person that I chose to live the rest of my life with.

The End

Leave your review. Your feedback helps me improve a lot!

TEASER: BIKER'S LOST BABY

BWWM Dark Mafia Romance

I didn't even know what I was doing at this party. It was for rich people only. That was why I was feeling so out of place. But my friend was here and she was supposed to help me with feeling better about this, and I couldn't see her anywhere.

To be honest, I didn't exactly enter the place where the party was happening yet. I was just outside the building, looking at it from side to side, and up and down, and imagining how it was possible that people built that place and made it look like what it was.

It was modern, fancy, luxurious, and pretty much every other adjective I could think of. The kind of place that made me think less about myself the moment I first stepped inside it, which I didn't know when it was going to happen. I could see some partygoers already leaving their cars to go to the party, and they were all laughing and chatting and having a blast.

As for me, I didn't even know if I was going to make it all the way to the party so that I could be with my friend. Since the place was mostly made of windows and glass doors, I was hoping I was going to see her from the outside, but there were also so many people... I just couldn't see her among them.

In the meantime, I was trying to control my breathing, and trying not to have too many crushes here in this place. The men that were coming to the party were so confident, so handsome, and so everything I liked that I just couldn't stop stealing glances at them, even though I knew I shouldn't be.

If there was something I promised myself when I was younger and I thought I could finally have a grasp on was what having a relationship was like, and I said I would never fall in love again with anyone.

I had just finished breaking up with my previous boyfriend and it was a nightmare. He thought he could control me, that he could do anything to me, and he was making my life a living hell. I was just so happy that he wasn't a part of it anymore, but that didn't change anything. I just kept thinking about him, thinking about how much he affected my life and also thinking about what I was going to do now without someone to help me.

The truth was that even though I had a stable job, it didn't pay me enough. Certainly not enough to pay the bills and the food and everything else I needed to survive.

Just thinking about that, I decided to shake my head and not think about those things anymore. One of the things I said I was going to do at this party was that I was going there, going to see my friend, and I was going to have a blast with her. After all, that was one of the things she promised we were going to do.

She had a better job than me. She was a fashion advisor and one of the best at it. Did I feel envious of it? Not at all, but it was something that made me think about my life and everything else that was associated with it. One of the things that I knew would never change, something I thought would never happen, but which did, was the fact that I had a son.

He was the most beautiful, sweet thing in the world, but I couldn't deny that he was also one of my sources of stress. Even though I knew he could be better, he wasn't – at least, not to me.

I didn't like thinking about him that way, so I shooed that thought out of my mind right at this moment.

He didn't make my life a living hell and it was better with

him around, but there was no denying that he was spoiled. I thought I wasn't helping with putting him in that direction, but it happened, and I couldn't do anything about it. I couldn't change it anymore.

No matter what I did, he was always going to look at me and wonder what happened to his father. He was going to keep asking me why I broke up with him, even though it was the only thing I could do at that moment so that I didn't explode.

Now, we were living in a very rundown and dingy apartment, and it was the kind of place I just didn't want to go back to. I left him with my mother, who was at least living with me and was helping me with taking care of the apartment.

But even then, that meant I also had to keep working so that I could keep putting food on the table and she didn't have to feel hungry. I loved her. She was my mother and I would do anything for her, and I was glad that she was helping me recently by taking care of my son when I was working and, some other times, going to places like this, but there was no denying that she also put some extra weight in my life.

I took a deep breath and decided to enter the building. A guard stood outside of it and he looked at me as though he knew I wasn't supposed to be here. But even if that was what he was thinking, I was going to prove him wrong.

After all, I did my best before coming here. I groomed myself, bought a different dress just for this party, did my hair, put on better makeup than what I had before, and also even bought better perfume so that the first thing that everyone thought about me was how good it smelled.

The guard was a tall man, with a cap, and he wore a mask, most likely because he was afraid of the pandemic. But just like everyone else, we had been jabbed several times, took all the doses, and we should all be protected against the virus.

That wasn't going to stop him, though, from wearing a mask at the party. He was one of the few that wore one. Everyone else going into the building didn't have masks on, and at least that was one of the few reasons why I didn't feel completely out of place yet.

I mean, I kind of did, but at least that was something I could relate to them.

He was also black, just like I was, though his skin tone was slightly darker than mine. I didn't think much about that, just that everyone else in the party, other than the guard, was white.

I supposed that was one of the few things that should have helped me to spot my friend among the partygoers. Considering that everyone here was white or mixed race, then another black woman among them should have helped me with finding her, right?

But it was also likely she was nowhere near the party. More often than not, she was late to do anything.

In the meantime, I just couldn't stop thinking about my son and if he was doing okay. I knew that he had some kind of condition that made him think differently. Sometimes, he behaved so weirdly. Sometimes, he acted as though he didn't even know who I was.

Sometimes, he also acted as though he couldn't see anything, even though I took him to the eye doctor so many times to check his eyes and she always told me that everything was okay with them.

"Your name, Ms.?" The guard asked, and I gave him my name, which he checked on the list he was holding in his hands. It was a white, single paper sheet with a list of names, and I knew that my name had to be on it. The problem was that I still couldn't stop feeling nervous, my fingers moving and twitching slightly. It was one of the things about me that always showed how nervous I was.

His eyes checked the list of names and then he looked at me and I gave him my ID. The first thing I thought was going to happen was that he wasn't going to find my name on the list, he was going to ask me to turn around and leave, and then I would ask my friend so many questions, pretty much cornering her, that I knew I would lose my friendship with her.

But then, he looked up, giving me my ID back. I put it back in my shoulder bag and then I smiled when he said, "You can go in, Ms. Crawford."

SIMILAR BOOKS

SERIES - ALPHA HUNTERS

1. Not my Wedding
2. Not my Vows
3. Not his Baby
4. Not my Fiancé
5. Not my Daughter

SERIES - RUTIILESS MAFIOSOS

1. His Accidental Triplets
2. His Sweet Captive
3. His Stolen Bride
4. His Accidental Baby
5. His Secret Triplets
6. His Fleeing Single Mom
7. Not my Daughter
8. Not my Fiancé

ABOUT THE AUTHOR

Ruthless mafiosos, gorgeous billionaires, and feisty heroines are just tiny fractions of Jolie Damman's stories. She breathes and lives dark romance, peppering each scene with intrigue and tension that sweep readers away.

When she isn't writing, she's reading by the fireplace of her house as she takes sips of her tea.